To Matt Cohen — A Z

Text copyright © 2001 by Teddy Jam
Illustrations copyright © 2001 by Ange Zhang

Groundwood Books/Douglas & McIntyre
720 Bathurst Street, Suite 500
Toronto, Ontario M5S 2R4

Distributed in the USA by Publishers Group West
1700 Fourth Street
Berkeley, CA 94710

We acknowledge the financial support of the Canada Council for the
Arts, the Ontario Arts Council and the Government of Canada
through the Book Publishing Industry Development Program for our
publishing activities.

ONTARIO ARTS COUNCIL
CONSEIL DES ARTS DE L'ONTARIO

National Library of Canada Cataloguing in Publication Data
Jam, Teddy
The kid line
A Groundwood book.
ISBN 0-88899-432-X
1. Conacher, Charlie, 1909-1967 — Juvenile fiction. I. Zhang, Ange.
II. Title.
PS8569.A427K52 2001   jC813'.54   C2001-930499-4
PZ7.J153567Ki 2001

Printed and bound in China by Everbest Printing Co. Ltd.

THE KID LINE

STORY BY

Teddy Jam

PICTURES BY

Ange Zhang

A GROUNDWOOD BOOK

DOUGLAS & McINTYRE • TORONTO VANCOUVER BUFFALO

WHEN he was young, my father worked on building Maple Leaf Gardens. "Right there," he'd say. "Look at that brick. I laid that brick. I remember." We'd be standing across the street when he pointed out his bricks, the ones he said he remembered.

Sometimes it would be winter, so dark and so cold that my feet were already frozen and I would be wanting to go home. Or it could be later in the year. March or April if the Leafs were in the playoffs.

December and April were my favorite months for hockey. December because I liked playing shinny in the park while the sky lost its blue, as though someone had just poured it out. Then the lights would come on and I'd be skating as fast as I could down the

rink, and with every cut of my blades against the ice I'd be thinking, Look out, Big Train.

Big Train was my father's favorite player. Big Train Lionel Conacher and his brother Charlie who played for the Leafs.

The Conacher brothers, when they were boys, went to Jesse
Ketchum Public School. So did my father after them. He played
hockey and football with them and talked about how it was to have
gotten run over by Big Train when he was only nine years old and
about how getting run over by Big Train was like getting driven over
by a cement truck even then, or so my father said.

After the Conacher brothers finished at Jesse Ketchum they became professional athletes, and my father could read their names in the papers. After my father finished school he started as an apprentice to a bricklayer, like his father, and he worked on Maple Leaf Gardens, which is where Charlie Conacher became a big star and led the league in scoring two times.

While Charlie Conacher was getting famous, my father built more buildings. After that he went to the war and he came back. My mother used to say the war had knocked my father off his tracks. Like he'd gotten hit by a Big Train, I used to think.

By the time I got old enough to know what my father did, what he did was sell tickets outside Maple Leaf Gardens on game night. I would go with him.

Other people who sold tickets would walk up and down outside the arena yelling out their seat locations and prices. They'd be wearing bright team windbreakers and sometimes wearing toques.

Not my father. "You look like a doctor," my mother would say. She was the family expert on fashion. She worked at the Eaton's store on College Street kitty-corner from the Gardens. Sometimes my father would meet her there for lunch, on his way to buy tickets for that night. He had a long wool coat and a movie star kind of hat that he'd pull down over his forehead as though he didn't want to be recognized. He had his corner where he always stood, away from the hustle, and sometimes in the very coldest weather he would drink coffee out of a thermos, coffee so thick with milk and sugar that I was also allowed a few gulps to warm up.

Halfway through the game we'd go home and listen to the rest of the game on the radio. Often a sports announcer or someone writing in the paper would say something about the Conacher brothers. Of course their playing days were over. Big Train had run for Parliament and Charlie had coached for a while. "Used to play with them," my father would say. He had a dreamy way of talking as though he'd decided his whole life was a dream.

One day we were skating, whirling around the rink, my father wearing his long overcoat the way he always did.

"I bet I can beat you," I said, and we raced around the rink, my father always a few strides behind as I beat him to the line I'd scratched across the ice. And then, as I was trying to catch my breath, my father made a little circle, taking off his coat so that he was just wearing the blue sweater he always brought skating, and suddenly he was off again, his arms swinging from side to side as he picked up speed until finally he was going so fast that I started to cry because I was afraid he wouldn't be able to stop.

One night I was standing a few steps away from my father while he was selling the last of his tickets. The game had already started and soon it would be time to go home. "Reds," I heard my father say. Reds were the best seats. "I haven't had any Reds for two hours. Nothing left but a few Greens." I looked up. My father was talking to a big man, unshaven. Sometimes, those very occasional times when my father had unsold tickets, we'd go and watch the game ourselves.

I couldn't hear what the man was offering my father, but I could see my father shrugging, as though he'd decided he'd rather use the tickets than sell them for so little. Then suddenly my father came up to me and said we were going inside, too, the three of us.

It was a March night. The Leafs were playing the Bruins and fighting for a playoff spot. By the time we got in, the Leafs were already down 2-1.

In those years Ted Kennedy was the Leafs' best player. Famous for his intensity, he had already helped the Maple Leafs win a Stanley Cup as part of the New Kid Line. The Old Kid Line, the first, had of course starred Charlie Conacher.

I was sitting between my father and the stranger. When the Bruins scored their third goal, the stranger gave a little grunt. One of his hands took hold of the seat in front of us, and I saw that his knuckles were huge and swollen, the way hockey players' knuckles get, my father had explained to me, either from fighting or getting hit with the puck.

Then I saw that the man had a big scar along one cheek, and another line that might have been a scar on his chin. I should have recognized him right away. Charlie Conacher. His picture was up in the hall of our school, and my father had shown me his Conacher brothers scrapbook a dozen times.

"Play hockey?" he now asked me.

"Just fool around," I said. "Do you?"

"Used to," he said. Then he asked, "Are you any good?"

"No," I admitted. "Even my father can skate faster than me."

"It's not how fast you go. It's what you do," the stranger said. "What's your position?"

"Used to be a forward," I said. "Now sometimes I have to play goalie."

"I was a goalie for a while."

That's when I knew he was Charlie Conacher. My father had told me about how he'd started off as a goalie, then used to carry the puck with his goalie stick until finally a coach let him play up front.

For the rest of the game I sat beside him. Every now and then he would clench his hands in frustration as the Leafs made a mistake or failed to score, and then, just before the end, he disappeared.

The whole way home my father didn't say anything, so I kept quiet until we were back in our kitchen and my mother was making us hot chocolate.

"You'll never guess who sat with us tonight," I said.

My father put the newspaper in front of his face.

"Charlie Conacher. I recognized him right away. His face was covered in scars."

"That's no way to talk about someone," my mother said. "I'm sure Charlie Conacher is a very nice man."

"He told me he used to play goal sometimes."

"I scored on him a couple of times," my father said.

That night I dreamed I was at the Gardens again. But in my dream, when the Leafs were down 3-1, Charlie Conacher stood up like a giant from the seat beside me, took a giant's step and landed on the ice wearing his old skates and his old Leaf sweater.

He looked lumpy and funny in his old uniform. His pads stuck out in crazy ways and he was still wearing the black cap he'd worn to the arena.

But as the Boston player tried to pass him, Charlie Conacher pushed him against the boards and took the puck away. Soon he was skating down the ice — not flying, but skating as fast as he could and doing something with the puck: keeping it.

Then, way over on the other side of the rink, I saw my father. He was skating, too, skating fast, skating faster than I'd ever seen him skate. He was wearing his overcoat and his hat and his scarf was flying and just as Charlie Conacher crossed the blue line, my father was sweeping in toward the goal.

I could see everything. I could see it perfectly because I was coming in behind them, slow but sure, tiny and unseen between the other players. I was cruising toward the goal with my stick out and

suddenly Charlie had passed it to my father who had passed it to me and I was all alone in front of this giant goaltender but his legs were open and I poked the puck between them.

My father stopped selling tickets when my parents moved into the old age home. He could still skate and once, when I took him to the rink with my daughter, he let her beat him as she scooted up and down the boards. He watched the Saturday night games on TV, though he always said the Leafs weren't as good as they used to be. Occasionally I would take him to a game.

Before the Gardens closed he liked to stand outside with me after
the game, watching the building go dark. Now I sometimes go down
there alone, at night. You can almost see the ghosts coming in and out,

almost hear their skates cutting up the ice, their shouts, their laughter. And then after they leave the building there's a long silence. It's something you can't hear, but you can remember.